PUFFIN BOOKS

Editor: Kaye Webb

LUCKY DIP

Ruth Ainsworth was an early writer for *Listen
with Mother* programmes on the radio, and
her stories and poems have long been estab-
lished favourites. She has exactly the eye-level
of the under-fives, whether it is in story or
verse, and whether she is telling of Charles and
his family, or animals, trains, motorcars, steam
rollers, or Christmas trees. And there are tales
of all these things in this volume. Each is
exactly right, and beautifully complete in itself,
for telling or reading aloud in a quiet space of
ten minutes or so. The choice and diversity
of subjects and the expert handling are guaran-
teed to give pleasure to the reader – and that
always adds to the delight of the listeners.

Here you will find seven of the best loved
Charles stories, eight completely new and
hitherto unpublished tales, and seven of the
verses which are asked for over and over again
– all from *Listen with Mother*.

LUCKY DIP

A SELECTION OF STORIES
AND VERSES
BY
RUTH AINSWORTH

ILLUSTRATED
BY
GERALDINE SPENCE

PUFFIN BOOKS

Puffin Books, Penguin Books Ltd, Harmondsworth, Middlesex, England
Penguin Books Inc., 7110 Ambassador Road, Baltimore, Maryland 21207, U.S.A.
Penguin Books Australia Ltd, Ringwood, Victoria, Australia
Penguin Books Canada Ltd, 41 Steelcase Road West, Markham, Ontario, Canada
Penguin Books (N.Z.) Ltd, 182–190 Wairau Road, Auckland 10, New Zealand

—

This selection first published in Puffin Books 1961
Reprinted 1963, 1965, 1966, 1969, 1971, 1973, 1975, 1976

—

This selection copyright © Puffin Books, 1961

'Charles' Useful Bag', 'Charles and the String Plait', and
'Charles Makes a House' are taken from *Listen with Mother
Tales*; 'Charles is Cross', 'Charles and Dapple', and ''The
Box under the Table' from *Charles Stories and Others*;
'Granny in the Country' from *More About Charles*. These
books are published by William Heinemann Ltd

—

Made and printed in Great Britain
by Hazell Watson & Viney Ltd,
Aylesbury, Bucks
Set in Monotype Imprint

Contents

Hob Nob

ONCE upon a time there was a red engine called Hob Nob. He had his name painted in black letters on the side.

Behind the engine was the tender. Behind the tender was a string of trucks – one, two, three, four, five, six trucks. At the end of the trucks was the guard's van.

'Puff – puff – puff!' said Hob Nob as he went along the lines. 'Puff – puff – puff!'

One day Hob Nob met a lamb.

'M-aaa!' said the lamb. 'Will you give me a ride to the fair?'

'Yes, I will,' said Hob Nob. 'Jump in.'

So the lamb jumped into the first truck.

Then Hob Nob met a dog.

'Bow-wow!' said the dog. 'Will you give me a ride to the fair?'

'Yes, I will,' said Hob Nob. 'Jump in.'

So the dog jumped into the second truck.

Then Hob Nob met a cat.

'Me-ow!' said the cat. 'Will you give me a ride to the fair?'

'Yes, I will,' said Hob Nob. 'Jump in.'

So the cat jumped into the third truck.

[8]

Then Hob Nob met a duck.

'Quack-quack!' said the duck. 'Will you give me a ride to the fair?'

'Yes, I will,' said Hob Nob. 'Jump in.'

So the duck jumped into the fourth truck.

[9]

Then Hob Nob met a hen.

'Cluck-cluck!' said the hen. 'Will you give me a ride to the fair?'

'Yes, I will,' said Hob Nob. 'Jump in.'

So the hen jumped into the fifth truck.

Then Hob Nob met a turkey.

'Gobble-gobble!' said the turkey. 'Will you give me a ride to the fair?'

'Yes, I will,' said Hob Nob. 'Jump in.'

So the turkey jumped into the sixth truck.

On they went – 'Puff – puff – puff – puff!' – with the lamb in the first truck, the dog in the second truck, the cat in the third truck, the duck in the fourth truck, the hen in the fifth truck, and the turkey in the sixth truck.

Soon they came to a tunnel, and the tunnel was dark and sooty black.

'M-aaa!' said the lamb. 'I don't like the black tunnel. I don't like its big black mouth. I think it will eat me up.'

'Bow-wow! Me-ow! Quack-quack! Cluck-cluck! Gobble-gobble!' said the dog, the cat, the duck, the hen, and the turkey, all together. 'We don't like the black tunnel either!'

'Never mind,' said Hob Nob. 'I will blow my

whistle when we go into the dark. I will make up my fire now, and send out sparks all the way through the tunnel. Then you won't be frightened.'

So he blew his whistle, 'Toot! Toot! Toot!' and he sent out lots of bright sparks, red ones and yellow ones. Then no one minded the black tunnel.

When Hob Nob got to the fair, he put on his brakes, and the tender and all the six trucks stopped. The lamb got out of the first truck, and the dog got out of the second truck, the cat got out of the third, the duck out of the fourth, the hen out of the fifth, and the turkey out of the sixth truck.

The lamb went on the roundabouts.

The dog went on the swings.

The cat went on the big dipper.

The duck had some candy floss.

The hen had an iced lolly.

The turkey had a drink of ginger pop.

Hob Nob had a nice nap in the sunshine, which was what he liked best.

So they ALL had fun.

The Snowman

WE look out of the window
To see the snowman stand
Cold and white
All day and night,
With an icicle in his hand.

The snowman looks in the window
To see us having our tea;
The fire burns red
As we eat our bread
And he thinks, 'How HOT they must be!'

The Little Donkey

A LITTLE donkey ran round and round a field. The little donkey was black and the field was green, but as the snow was falling, both the donkey and the field were covered with white snowflakes.

The little donkey was not cold, but he was lonely. There was no other donkey to talk to. When he threw back his head and said, 'Hee-haw!' there was no friendly voice to say 'Hee-haw!' back again.

Two little girls looked over the gate into the field. 'Good night,' they called to the donkey. 'We can't stop. We must hurry home and hang up our stockings.'

'Why do you want to hang up your stockings?' asked the little donkey.

'Because it's Christmas Eve and Father Christmas will come tonight and fill them with toys.'

'Who is Father Christmas?' asked the little donkey.

'He is a kind old man with a white beard and a red coat and a hood with fur round it,' said one little girl.

'He drives a sledge pulled by reindeer,' said the other little girl. 'And he has a sack of toys on the sledge, and he puts them into the stockings he finds hanging up at the foot of children's beds.'

'He must be *very* kind,' said the little donkey. 'Does he only bring presents to children? Never to donkeys?'

'We don't know,' said the little girls. 'Perhaps. Good night, and a happy Christmas!'

The little donkey stopped running round his snowy field, and stood still and thought. He wished Father Christmas would drive his sledge that way, and give him a present out of the big sack. He did not mind what sort of a present it was. Anything would do. He had never heard of stockings and Christmas presents before, and he was sure he would like them very much, whatever they might be.

In the middle of that night, the little donkey woke to hear the sound of bells ringing. He opened his eyes and saw a beautiful silver sledge drawn by four reindeer skimming over the snow. It was driven by a man with a white beard and a red coat. A red hood was pulled snugly over his head, and it was trimmed with fur as white as his beard.

'It must be Father Christmas,' thought the little donkey. Then he saw a big, bulging sack on the sledge, and knew he was right.

The sledge stopped in the field, and the little donkey could see Father Christmas's merry blue eyes and rosy-red cheeks.

'We're in trouble,' he said as he got off the sledge. 'Springer, my youngest reindeer, has gone lame. I shall have to unharness her and let her rest, but the sledge is so heavy that I don't think the other three can pull it alone. Will you help? You look strong, though you are small.'

'Of course I will,' cried the little donkey, jumping up and frisking his tail. 'And Springer can rest in my shed, and lie on my bed of straw.'

So Father Christmas led the poor lame reindeer into the shed, and made her comfortable on the soft straw. Then he harnessed the little donkey in her place, next to a reindeer called Racer, behind the other two, Lightning and Leaper.

Father Christmas jumped on the sledge, shook the reins, and off they went. The silver bells on the harness jingled and the little donkey felt as light as a feather. He flew with the reindeer through the air, over the roof-tops, over the tree-tops, and over the church steeples. Then they came down to earth again, and Father Christmas took the sack of toys on his back and went into the houses where there were children in bed and fast asleep. He filled their stockings with just the things they wanted most.

He visited the house where the two little girls lived, the ones who had wished the little donkey a happy Christmas. They were asleep in bed. He stuffed an apple in the toe of each stocking, then some nuts and an orange. After that he put in a string of beads, a fairy doll, and a tea-set wrapped in tissue paper. Neither of the little girls woke because Father Christmas stepped as softly as a cat with furry paws.

At last the sack was empty, and the stockings hanging on the beds were full. The little donkey had enjoyed every minute of it, but he was getting tired, and he was glad when he saw that they were coming down at last in his own field.

Springer was much better for the rest, and hardly limped at all.

'You have been a great help,' said Father Christmas, stroking the little donkey's neck with a warm hand. 'You deserve a big Christmas present. What would you like?'

'I should like a friend, please,' said the little donkey at once. 'I have to play all by myself now, and I go to bed alone in my shed at night.'

'Sleep soundly then,' said Father Christmas smiling, 'and in the morning, look for your surprise.'

The sledge rose in the air and sailed away, the silver bells ringing, and the reindeer crying back, 'Happy Christmas! Happy Christmas!'

Next morning, when the little donkey woke up, the first thing he saw when he opened his eyes was a little white donkey standing in the doorway of his shed.

'Hee-haw! A Happy Christmas!' said the white donkey.

'Happy Christmas!' cried the little black donkey. 'Who are you?'

'My name is Snow Queen,' said the white donkey, 'and I have come to be your friend, and play with you, and share your straw bed at night.'

They rubbed noses and then galloped round and round the field till they were tired. Then they told each other stories in the shed till they were rested.

The two little girls came along and brought them some carrots for a Christmas treat.

'But look!' one of them cried. 'There are two donkeys now!'

'Then Father Christmas must have brought the little black donkey a present as well!' laughed the other little girl. 'And there are enough carrots for two! Isn't that a good thing?'

So both the black donkey and the white donkey had a happy Christmas.

Charles' Useful Bag

THERE was once a little boy called Charles who liked collecting things. Sometimes he collected acorns. Sometimes he collected chestnuts. Sometimes he collected bus tickets. His pockets were always full of whatever he was collecting at the time. His mother gave him a big brown paper bag to put his things in, but the bag soon broke because he filled it too full.

One day, Charles' grandmother made him a bright blue bag with a piece of tape threaded in the top, so he could draw the tape tight and close the bag safely. It was a large, strong bag. She sewed some words on the bag in white cotton and the words read: MY USEFUL BAG.

Charles loved his Useful Bag. It was nearly as big as a sack. Just then he was collecting fir-cones and every afternoon his mother took him into a little wood, where fir trees grew. There were lots of fir-cones lying on the ground and

Charles picked up all he could see and put them into his bright blue bag.

'Whatever will you do with all those fir-cones?' asked his mother.

'Whatever will you do with all those fir-cones?' asked his father.

'Whatever will you do with all those fir-cones?' asked the milkman and the postman and the baker.

'I don't know,' said Charles, 'but they will come in useful one day.' And he went on picking up fir-cones and dropping them into his bright blue bag. Soon the bag was nearly full.

One afternoon Charles was going to the wood with his mother, when he saw an old man sitting by a hedge. The old man had made a little fire and he was holding a frying-pan over the fire and cooking some bacon in it. The fire looked as if it would go out any minute. There were no flames, only a curl of grey smoke.

'Why doesn't your bacon spit and sizzle like our bacon does at home?' asked Charles.

'Because my fire is so small,' said the old man. 'If I had a big, hot fire, my bacon would spit and sizzle like yours.'

'I will make your fire hot,' said Charles, and he undid the tape round the mouth of his bag and tipped out all his fir-cones.

The old man put the fir-cones on the fire; first a small handful, then a bigger handful, then more and more till the fire burned bright and the bacon spat and sizzled.

'Thank you very much,' said the old man. 'Now my bacon will taste crisp and good. I have something in my pocket I should like to give you.'

He put his hand into his pocket and brought out a little wooden boat. It had two masts and a rudder.

'I made this myself with my knife,' he said. 'You can sail it in your bath.'

Charles thanked the old man very much and that night he sailed the wooden boat in his bath. It sailed very well. He made little waves with his hands and even then it did not upset. It was the best boat he had ever had.

The Middle of the Night

THE house was very quiet because it was the middle of the night. The father and mother were asleep. The children were asleep. The cat was asleep on the rug in the kitchen, and the dog was asleep in his basket.

Upstairs, in the corner of the children's bedroom, behind a cupboard, low down between the wall and the floor, there was a little dark hole. In this dark hole lived two mice. That night, one little mouse woke up suddenly and rubbed his eyes with his paws and yawned.

'What was that?' he said to his sister-mouse.

Then the sister-mouse woke up, and rubbed her eyes with her paws, and yawned.

'What was what?' she said.

'I thought it was bells ringing,' said the brother-mouse.

'That must have been what woke me too,' said his sister. 'I thought I heard bells ringing and feet galloping.'

If they had come out of their hole, and had climbed up by the curtain and looked out of the window, they would have seen what woke them. A sledge drawn by reindeer with bells round their necks had come gliding over the roof-tops. But the little mice stayed in their hole, rubbing their eyes and yawning.

'I am very hungry,' said brother-mouse. 'I could eat anything. I could eat the stalest crumbs, or any old scrap of bacon fat.'

'So could I,' said the sister-mouse. 'I could nibble a bit of old potato, or the top of a carrot.'

'Let's go and see what we can find,' said the brother-mouse. 'There may be something good for supper lying about. But keep close to me.'

The two little mice crept out of their hole, and began to scamper this way and that, over the bedroom floor, in search of something good to eat. Their noses twitched when they smelled floor polish, but it did not smell good to eat. Soon the brother-mouse came to the foot of the bed. A stocking was hanging down from the bed-post – and it was packed full of something. It was fat and lumpy, and good smells came from it.

'Sister! Come quickly,' he squeaked. 'I've found a long woollen stocking, and it is stuffed full of things that smell good.'

'What is it stuffed with?' asked the sister-mouse.

'I don't know,' he said, sniffing, 'but it smells like a good supper. Come and sniff for yourself.'

So the sister-mouse scampered across to him, and they both stood up on their little back legs, and they both sniffed together.

'Apples!' squealed brother-mouse.

'Oranges!' squeaked sister-mouse.

'Nuts!' they shrieked together.

'If we nibble a hole up there, we could get at them,' said brother-mouse.

So they began to nibble the toe of the stocking with their sharp teeth and out fell a round, rosy apple. They ran after it and found that one side of the apple was rosy and one side was yellow. They began to nibble with small quick bites, and their little teeth marks were like the scratches made by a very small saw. Brother-mouse nibbled the rosy side of the apple, and sister-mouse nibbled the yellow side, but the red tasted as good as the yellow, and the yellow every bit as good as the red. The juice ran out as they nibbled, and they licked it up with their tiny, pointed tongues. When they had eaten nearly enough apple, they heard a voice inside the stocking saying:

'Let me out! Let me out!'

They stood up on tiptoe again and with their teeth pulled the hole a little wider, and out came a pink sugar mouse with a piece of string for a tail.

'Oh, thank you,' said the pink sugar mouse. 'I am one of your cousins, did you know?'

'You haven't any fur,' said the brother-mouse.

'That is because I am made of sugar,' said the pink mouse.

'You can't whisk your tail like we do,' said sister-mouse.

'Perhaps not,' said the pink mouse. 'I haven't tried. But I am very sweet.'

'Why do you live in that long woollen stocking?' they both asked.

'Oh, I don't live there. I am a Christmas sugar mouse. Father Christmas brought me on his sledge with the apple and the orange and the nuts and toys. We are all Christmas presents for Lucy, the little girl who is asleep in that bed.'

'Oh dear!' cried brother-mouse. 'We've been eating Lucy's Christmas apple!'

'Oh dear!' cried sister-mouse. 'I have eaten all the yellow off!'

'And we've made a hole in her stocking,' said brother-mouse.

'Whatever shall we do?' they both wailed together, and they began to cry because they were kind little mice.

Now the sugar mouse was very sensible, even though her tail was made of string.

'We can't do anything about the apple,' she said, 'so you had better finish it between you. But we can mend the hole. One of Lucy's Christmas presents is a sewing box. I will fetch it out.'

She leapt up, into the toe of the stocking, and brought out a box with a lid you could see through. Inside were tiny reels of white cotton, and black and red. They were no bigger than acorns. There was a thimble, and a row of needles stuck in a piece of white flannel. The thimble was too big, but the sugar mouse managed to thread the needle with black cotton. Then the

three mice lifted up the sewing box and pushed it back through the toe of the stocking, and the pink mouse jumped in after it and sewed up the hole behind her. She did it so neatly that it hardly showed. Before she sewed up the very last little bit of the hole, she called down:

'Good-bye, little mice! Happy Christmas!'

In the morning Lucy woke before it was light,

and felt at once for her stocking. There it was, hanging on the end of the bed, fat and heavy. Father Christmas had not forgotten her. There was a lamp beside her bed, and she turned on the light. Then she pulled the stocking up over the quilt, and began to open it.

First, a sprig of holly had to be taken out of the top. Below it were little parcels in gay paper wrappings. She found the sewing set, and the sugar mouse, and an orange, and some nuts, and she did not even look for an apple. Later on, Lucy's mother found the apple core on the floor and said:

'Lucy would never eat an apple and throw the core on the floor!' And when she picked it up, she saw the tiny tooth marks on it.

'Now I wonder what that means!' she said.

'It looks as though a mouse had nibbled it,' said Lucy.

'But there are no mice in *this* house,' said her mother, '– except sugar ones.'

'Squeak! Squeak! Squeak!' said two tiny little voices from under the cupboard. 'That's what you think!'

Acorn Bill

I MADE a little acorn man
And inked his smiling face,
I stuck four pins for legs and arms,
Each firmly in its place.

I found a tiny acorn cup
To put upon his head,
And then I showed him to my friends:
'Meet Acorn Bill,' I said.

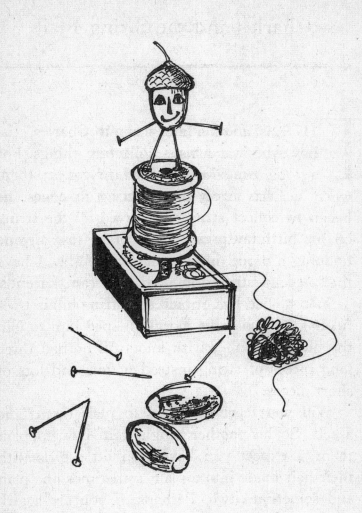

Charles and the String Plait

THIS is another story about Charles, the boy who was always collecting things. For a long time he collected fir-cones; then, when he was tired of collecting fir-cones, he began to collect string. He saved all the string off his birthday presents and if he saw anyone undoing a parcel he always asked: 'May I have that piece of string, please, if you can spare it?'

Soon he had lots of pieces of string in his Useful Bag. One day his mother helped him to join the pieces together with knots till he had three long pieces of string instead of lots and lots of short pieces.

'Will you teach me how to plait them?' he asked. So his mother taught him how to plait them. I expect you have seen little girls with their hair made into a plait, sometimes one plait and sometimes two. Perhaps, if you are a girl, you have plaits yourself.

Charles' plait grew longer and longer till he

had used up all the three pieces of string and made them into a string plait rather like a rope.

'Whatever will you do with your string plait?' asked Mother.

'Whatever will you do with your string plait?' asked Father.

'Whatever will you do with your string plait?' asked the milkman and the postman and the baker.

'I don't know,' said Charles, 'but it will come in useful one day.' Wherever he went he carried the string plait in his pocket.

One morning he was out shopping with Mother and suddenly a little black-and-white puppy ran right across the busy road. The cars put on their brakes – squeak! squeak! The buses blew their horns – poop! poop! People on bicycles rang their bells – ting-a-ling! ting-a-ling! The little black-and-white puppy yelped with fright – yelp! yelp!

Then a little girl ran to the puppy and took him up in her arms and stroked him and comforted him. 'You must not go on to the road,' she said. 'You might get hurt.'

'Is he your puppy?' asked Charles' mother.

'Yes,' said the little girl. 'I have bought him a collar but I have lost his lead. And he is so lively that he won't stay on the path and I am afraid he may get run over.'

'I can give you a lead,' said Charles. 'A good, strong lead. Then he will be safe.' He put his hand in his pocket and brought out his string plait.

'Thank you,' said the little girl. 'It is just what I wanted.'

Charles' mother fastened one end to the puppy's collar and the little girl held the other end in her hand. They went off together, the little girl smiling and the black-and-white puppy frisking about on his new lead.

Charles was happy too. His string plait had come in useful after all.

One, Two

ONE, two,
What shall I do?

Three, four
Play on the floor.

Five, six,
Build with bricks.

Seven, eight,
Make a gate.

Nine, ten,
Knock it down again.

The Box Under the Table

TWO kittens lived with their mother in a box under the kitchen table. One was called Pansy because her face was like a black, crumpled pansy. She was a good little kitten. The other was called Tip because he had a white tip to his tail. He was a bad little kitten. Their mother, Minnie, loved them both and thought they were the best kittens in the world.

The kitchen belonged to a woman in a white apron called Mrs Plum. She swept and dusted and poked the fire and rattled the pots and pans. Sometimes she filled a pail with soapy water and scrubbed the floor. When this happened, she lifted up the box with the kittens inside and put it on the kitchen table, so it should not get wet. Then the kittens had a good view of the whole kitchen. The dresser with the cups and saucers in neat rows. The clock on the mantelpiece. The shining brass door-handle. Everything.

'How big the world is,' said Tip, peeping over the edge of the box while Mrs Plum scrubbed the floor. 'One day I shall explore every corner. Will you come with me?'

'I don't know,' said little Pansy. 'I am afraid of the monster with red tongues who lives inside the kitchen stove and eats lumps of coal. He roars and crackles.'

'*I* am not afraid of him,' said Tip bravely. 'I shall go right up to him and spit, like this – P-t-t! P-t-t! Then *he* will be afraid of *me*. I shall growl, too, like this – G-r-r! G-r-r!'

That morning, after the floor was dry, Mrs Plum put some milk into a saucer and lifted the kittens out of the box and stood them on the floor, one each side of the saucer. 'You must learn to drink milk like your mother,' said Mrs Plum. 'Minnie! Minnie! Come and show your children how to lap milk.'

Minnie came out from the brush cupboard where she had been watching a mouse hole and her green eyes shone when she saw the milk. She stretched her neck till her mouth was level with the saucer and her pink tongue flicked in and out, flick – flick – flick – and she lapped the milk. 'Now, my kittens, you try to lap,' she said. 'It is quite easy.'

Tip put his nose in too far and sneezed, A-tish-oo! A-tish-oo! and spluttered milk over the clean floor, but Minnie quickly licked it up before Mrs Plum noticed. Pansy got on a little better. She curved her tiny tongue and tried to flick it in and out and lap up the milk.

'You are very slow,' said Minnie. 'Now I am going into the garden to sharpen my claws on the apple tree. When I come in I hope the saucer will be empty. One day, when you can drink milk properly, I will take you into the garden and show you many wonderful things.'

Minnie padded softly out of the kitchen.

'I don't like this horrid cold milk,' said Tip. 'Do you?'

'Not very much,' sighed Pansy, 'and I am tired of trying to lap.'

'Let's paddle in the milk,' said naughty Tip and he stood right in the middle of the saucer. When he got out, each paw left a milky mark like a star on the floor. Pansy paddled next and then her paws left milky stars as well. They pattered all over the floor leaving milky foot-prints everywhere.

Tip stopped by the coal scuttle and looked inside. 'I shall try some of this coal,' he said. 'The fire-monster eats lots of it every day, so it should be nice.' He licked a black lump till his tongue was as black as the coal.

'Is it good?' asked Pansy.

'It tastes very odd,' said Tip, licking away. 'Perhaps I shall be able to crackle and roar when I have eaten enough.'

Just then they heard creak – creak – creak and thud – thud – thud. This was Mrs Plum coming downstairs. The kittens scampered across the floor and scrambled into their box.

'What a mess!' said Mrs Plum, looking at the milky footmarks. 'I'll give you what-for.'

The kittens did not know what 'what-for' meant, but it sounded like something horrid, so they shut their eyes and pretended to be asleep.

When Minnie came in from the garden she was shocked to see the mess her kittens had made.

'It is no good snoring,' she said crossly. 'I know you are only pretending to be asleep. Now wake up and let me wash you properly.' She

started on Pansy and washed her from the tip
of her pansy nose to the tip of her tail. Then came
Tip's turn. He wriggled and squiggled and
squeaked, but it was no good. Minnie held him
firmly down with one paw and washed his ears
and between his dusty little toes and everywhere.

'Tomorrow you must have another try with a
saucer of milk,' said Minnie. 'Don't you want to
grow into cats and climb trees and catch mice
and sharpen your claws on the apple tree?'

'Yes, we do,' said Tip and Pansy.

'Mother, tell me what "what-for" is?' asked
Tip. 'Mrs Plum said she would give it to us if
we were naughty.'

'Well,' said Minnie, 'it might be a smack or it
might be a shake. Or it might be both. I hope
you will never find out.'

The kittens hoped so too, and they made up
their minds to be very good indeed.

Dot's Bicycle

DOT had a tricycle. It was very old. Once upon a time it had been her big brother's tricycle. Then it had been her big sister's tricycle. Now it was her tricycle. She had had it since she was very little, and now she was getting too big for it.

Dot's tricycle was the best thing she had ever had. She played with it for hours and hours. It would go UP steep slopes. It would go DOWN steep slopes. It would turn sharp corners. It would go fast or slow. She hardly ever fell off because it was so safe. But now she was getting too big for it.

One day, her uncle wrote a letter to her. The letter said he was going to give her a bicycle for her birthday.

Dot could not speak, she was so surprised and delighted. How lovely it would be to have a bicycle of her own, a brand new bicycle! Though she was silent, the others had plenty to say.

Her father said: 'But Dot always leaves her tricycle out in the rain.'

Her mother said: 'She even leaves it outside in the road.'

Her big brother said: 'I've seen it in the hen-run with the hens sitting on it.'

Her big sister said: 'I've seen it upside down beside the dustbin.'

Dot hung her head. Her face was very red. What they said was all quite true. She hardly ever remembered to put her tricycle away in the shed.

Then her father said: 'I've never seen Dot oil her tricycle.'

And her mother said: 'I've never seen her even dust it.'

Her big brother said: 'The bell doesn't ring. It's broken.'

Her big sister said: 'There isn't a scrap of paint left on it.'

Dot hung her head and her face went even redder. What they said was all quite true. She did not take any care of her tricycle.

'Perhaps she should wait till she is older,' said her father.

'Uncle can give it to her next year,' said her mother.

'Tell Uncle *I* need a new bicycle to go to school on,' said her big brother.

But her big sister saw the tears in Dot's eyes, and said:

'Let her have it. It's Uncle's present and it is her birthday.'

So the bicycle came from the shop, in a van, on her birthday morning. It was blue. And Dot's father and mother, and big brother, and big sister, soon found they were ALL WRONG. They were wrong as wrong could be.

Dot never left her bicycle in the rain, or on the road, or in the hen-run, or upside down beside the dustbin.

She cleaned it, and oiled it, and dusted it regularly; and the hooter hooted, and for a long time there was not one single scratch on the beautiful blue paint.

After she had had it for weeks and weeks, people still said:

'Look at that beautiful bicycle! It must be *brand new*!'

'You see,' said Dot, 'this one was all my own,

my very own. It wasn't old when I had it like the tricycle. It was brand new, and beautiful, and shiny, every bit of it. So of course I take care of it.'

Charles Makes a House

CHARLES was very fond of making houses. Sometimes he made a house under the nursery table. Sometimes he put a rug over two chairs and made a house that way. Sometimes he crept inside the toy cupboard and *nearly* shut the door, leaving just a crack showing, and that made a small, dark, secret little house.

One day, when Charles was playing in the garden, he saw a hole at the foot of a tree, between two of the big roots. It was large enough to put both his hands inside. 'What a dear little house that hole would make,' he thought. 'Not for me, of course, but for some very small creature.'

He found some moss under the ferns on the rockery and made a green, mossy carpet for the floor. Then he picked a toadstool and stood it in the middle for a table. He scattered rose petals on the carpet to look pretty and smell nice.

Charles had a sand-pit in another part of the garden and he fetched some sand in his seaside pail and made a sandy path, leading to the door. Just outside the door he put a tin lid filled with water, so that anyone living in the house could have a drink when he wanted.

There were some other little holes between the roots of the tree and these would do nicely for cupboards and store-places. In one he put a pile of twigs, broken into tiny pieces for firewood. In another he put some good things to eat like parsley and mint and a pod of peas.

When it was time to go to bed, Charles did not want to leave his little house. He lay down flat on the ground and looked right inside and he wished he were small enough to live there. The mossy floor was so green and soft and the rose petals were such a pretty pink.

The next morning, after breakfast, Charles ran down the garden to see if the house was all right. He peeped inside the door. It looked just the same, very cosy but quite, quite empty. He did wish someone were living there.

He scattered some fresh petals on the floor and watered the moss with his watering-can, to keep it green and damp.

The next morning, after breakfast, Charles ran down the garden again to see if the house was all right. This time, as he peeped inside, he saw a little, shining, silvery track on the floor. Someone had crept up the sandy path and round the toadstool table, over the rose petals. It must have been a snail, because a snail always leaves a silvery track behind him.

But the snail had gone away. The little house was quite, quite empty again.

'Anyhow,' thought Charles, 'snails carry their houses on their backs. They don't need to live in *my* little house.'

He scattered some fresh petals on the floor and watered the moss with his watering-can, to keep it green and damp.

The next morning, after breakfast, Charles ran down the garden to see if the little house was all right. He peeped inside the door and a small, brown face with very bright eyes peeped out at him. It was a frog. It gave Charles a friendly look and then hopped slowly away.

The moss and the petals were quite flat, so perhaps the frog had slept there all night.

Charles' mother wrote FROG HOUSE on a strip of paper and pinned it on the tree, just above the door.

Charles was so happy that someone was living in his house. He watered the moss every day to keep it fresh, and scattered new petals on the floor. He hoped the friendly frog would often sleep there and perhaps paddle in the tin lid of water.

My Special House

A HIVE for a honey bee,
  A kennel for a dog,
A hutch for a rabbit
  And a pond for a frog.
A stable for a donkey,
  A hole for a mouse,
But I would like a caravan
  For my special house.

The Old Car

'CHUG! Chug! Chug!' said the old car as it went slowly up the hill. The car was very old, and the hill was very steep. The car went slowly, slowly, slowly. When it was almost at the top of the hill, it stopped. And it could not go any farther. It was stuck there.

A man with a case came walking up the hill, and the old car said to him:

'Oh man with a case,
Please stop, please stop,
Give me a push
And I'll get to the top.'

'I can't stop and give you a push,' said the man with the case. 'It would make me late at the office. Good-bye!'

Then a lady in white came up the hill, and the old car said:

'Oh lady in white,
Please stop, please stop,

Give me a push

And I'll get to the top.'

'I can't stop and give you a push,' said the lady in white. 'I should get my dress dirty. Good-bye!'

Then a big boy with a bag full of books came up the hill, and the old car said:

'Oh boy with the books,

Please stop, please stop,

Give me a push

And I'll get to the top.'

'I can't stop and give you a push,' said the big boy. 'I don't want to be late for school. Good-bye!'

Then a big girl with a bunch of flowers came up the hill, and the old car said:

'Oh girl with the flowers,

Please stop, please stop,

Give me a push

And I'll get to the top.'

'I can't stop and give you a push,' said the big girl. 'I might spoil my flowers. Good-bye!'

Then some little children came up the hill. They were too small to go to school. They were going to play in the park, and they had bats and balls and skipping ropes with them.

The old car did not ask *them* to give him a push. They were so small. But they all stopped and said:

'Are you stuck? Shall we give you a push?'

'You are too small to give me a push,' said the old car.

'We'll show you whether we're too small!' said the children. 'There are ten of us and if we all push hard, we'll get you to the top of the hill.'

Then the children put down their bats and balls and skipping ropes, and pushed, and pushed, and pushed, and pushed, all together.

'One – two – three – PUSH!' they shouted, and they all pushed.

'One – two – three – PUSH!'

And the old car began to rock, and then to move very, very slowly up the hill. Then it went a little quicker, and at last it was at the top of the hill.

'Oh thank you,' said the old car. 'Now jump in all of you, and I'll give you a ride down the other side of the hill to the park.'

So the children fetched their bats, and balls, and skipping ropes, and jumped in. There was just room for them all, as they were so small. The old car went downhill without pushing— chug, chug, chug — right down to the park, and stopped at the park gates.

'Good-bye, and thank you,' said the children. 'Thank you for a lovely ride.'

'Thank you!' said the old car. 'Thank you for giving me a push up the hill.'

Charles is Cross

IT was a damp, dull morning, and Charles was feeling dull too.

'I don't know what to do,' he complained. 'There's nothing in all the whole world I want to do.'

'Let's try to think of something,' said his mother. 'The rain has stopped. Why don't you put on your wellingtons and play in the garden?'

Charles' wellingtons were red and he was very fond of them, but on this particular day he felt cross and contrary.

'I'll play in the garden,' he said. 'But not in my wellingtons.'

'What a pity,' said his mother. 'You'll have to play indoors instead. The garden is far too wet for shoes.'

'I don't care,' said Charles. 'I like indoors best.' This was not really true, but he was cross.

He got out his colouring book and began to colour a very nice picture of a train. He snatched up the crayons and pressed so hard that he broke a green one doing the engine, and a red one doing the signal, and a blue one doing the sky. He broke a yellow one doing the sun, and a black one doing the smoke. So they were all broken.

Then he pulled his brick box out from under the table and began to build a tall tower. He piled the bricks just anyhow. Sometimes a large one. Then a small one. Then a wide one. Then a narrow one. The tower rocked and swayed and fell down with a crash.

The sun came out and shone through the window and Charles could see millions of specks of dust dancing in a sunbeam. How lovely it would be in the garden. But he had said he would not wear his wellingtons and he was still too cross to change his mind.

Mother brought him his orange juice and a biscuit.

'I don't want any elevenses,' said Charles.

'Very well,' said his mother, putting the juice and the biscuit back in the larder. Charles felt sorry he had not drunk his juice because he was thirsty, but he did not feel like asking to have it brought back.

'Now it is time for your rest,' went on his mother.

'I won't go to sleep. I won't *ever* go to sleep.'

'Never mind. You can stay awake. People can rest without going to sleep.'

Still grumbling, Charles stumped upstairs, thump, thump, thump, and mother took off his shoes and tucked him under the blankets.

'I won't lie down. I'll sit up.'

'Very well. You can rest sitting up.'

Charles sat up in his blue dressing-gown, looking very wide awake.

'Here is your useful bag,' said his mother, handing him the special bag Granny had made for his treasures. 'I've put a surprise in it.'

Every day at rest time, Charles' mother put a surprise in his useful bag. It was not anything new, not just bought at the shops. It was just one of his own toys that he had not played with lately. He always looked forward to plunging his hand deep into the bag and fumbling about till he had found the special thing.

Today, when he fumbled about, he found his monkey-glove inside. It was a little, soft monkey head with two little monkey arms, shaped like a glove. He could put his hand inside and when he moved his fingers and thumb, the monkey nodded and moved his arms. Charles loved his monkey-glove and he and monkey had long talks together. Of course he had to talk *for* monkey, but he used a special squeaky voice and they got on very well.

'Hallo, monkey,' said Charles.

'Hallo, Charles,' said monkey.

'Where have you been all this time?'

'I've been climbing a coconut tree to get coconuts.'

'Did you find any?'

'Yes. I found a hundred. I drank the milk and ate so much nut that I got hiccoughs.'

Charles felt rather sleepy, but he still sat up.

'Are you tired, monkey?'

'Yes, Charles. Very, very tired.'

'Then let's lie down.'

Charles and monkey snuggled down together.

'Shall I say "Peter Piper" to you, monkey?'

'Yes please.'

But before Charles got to the part about the pickled peppers, he was fast asleep and he slept till the cuckoo clock on the wall called 'Cuckoo' once.

That meant one o'clock and as he opened his eyes, his mother came in to wake him. He washed his hands and went downstairs with monkey to have dinner.

'Oh what a lovely dinner! A bird's nest,' said Charles, which was his name for a poached egg sitting in a nest of mashed potatoes.

Then came pancakes with sugar and lemon. Charles felt happy again and when he had listened to a story on the wireless, he got ready for his walk.

'I'll put my wellingtons on myself,' said Charles cheerfully and he pulled and tugged and got them on with no help.

'Can monkey come for a walk?'

'Yes, of course he can,' said mother. So Charles wore monkey-glove on one hand and a knitted one on the other.

As Charles splashed through the puddles, he talked to monkey.

'Wasn't I cross this morning?'

'Oh you were cross,' agreed monkey. 'Cross as two sticks.'

'I was as cross as TWENTY sticks. But I'm not cross now. I don't think I shall ever be cross again.'

'Oh goody! goody!' squeaked monkey, nodding his little monkey head and waving his paws, which showed he was happy.

The Steam Roller

THERE once was a Steam Roller who lived in a shed. The door had a padlock on it to keep the Steam Roller safe at night. A man named Fred took care of him in the day. Fred kept the key of the padlock in his pocket. Sometimes Fred wiped him with an oily rag. Sometimes he cleaned out his funnel with a long, black brush.

The Steam Roller had two wheels at the back and a big, heavy, round roller at the front. The wheels and the roller were made of iron. He had a boiler with three brass bands round it. The boiler was kept full of water. When Fred lit a fire under the boiler, the Steam Roller moved along, clank – clank – clank – puffing smoke out of his funnel. Fred steered him the way he had to go with a steering wheel.

Every day at eight o'clock Fred undid the padlock with the key out of his pocket, and opened the doors of the shed. He gave the Steam Roller his breakfast of coal. Then they set out to work together. Clank – clank – clank – went the Steam Roller. They helped a gang of men to mend holes in the road. When the holes had been filled in with bits of stone, the Steam Roller crushed them down with his big, heavy roller. To and fro he went, backwards and forwards, making the rough patch smooth and tidy.

The cars and lorries passing could only use half of the road when the Steam Roller was rolling the other half. A man with two flags stood in the road. When he waved the *green* flag, the cars and lorries could go on. When he waved his *red* flag, they had to stop and wait. If there were any children in the cars, they did not mind waiting. They liked to see the Steam Roller at work. They did not want to go on when the man waved his green flag.

The Steam Roller often wished he were a car or a lorry. They went on and on, over the hills and out of sight. He only went up and down, up and down, clank – clank – clank, crushing the stones. At the end of the day the holes in the road were neatly filled up and Fred and the Steam Roller were tired. The Steam Roller went back to his shed and Fred turned the key in the padlock and went home to his supper.

One day, the Steam Roller made up his mind to run away. He needed a holiday. He longed to go anywhere he pleased, and to see what was to be seen there, and to do just whatever he liked. He was tired of going to and fro in one place. But how could he get out of the shed when he was locked in and the padlock was on the door? – and the key of the padlock was in Fred's pocket?

One evening, Fred was in a hurry to get home to his supper, and he did not turn the key properly in the lock. So, when the Steam Roller woke up very early next morning and pushed against the doors of the shed, they burst open. Then clank, clank, over went his wheels, and out he rolled on to the road. There was no Fred to steer him. No Fred to make him work. No Fred to drive him to and fro, to and fro, in one place. He was really free to please himself for once.

It was so very early that there was no one else on the road. The Steam Roller had it all to himself. Cows put their heads over the hedges and stared. Sheep stared as well, and horses, and a goat. They had never in their lives seen a steam roller clanking by so early in the morning – and with no driver up in the little seat.

The father and mother rabbits brought their babies to the doors of their burrows to see the sight. 'Be good, little rabbits, and do what you are told,' they warned the little ones, 'or the big steam roller will take you away with him!' But the Steam Roller only smiled at them and went on, clank – clank – clank.

Soon the Steam Roller was tired of the hard road, and wanted to go over soft green fields for a change. Just then, he saw a field full of thistles. They grew as green and thick as grass. 'I will go across this lovely green field,' said the Steam Roller to himself and he turned off the hard road and rolled straight through the hedge.

The Steam Roller did not mind the prickles on the thistles because he was made of iron. He could not feel even a tickle from them. They were so much softer than the sharp stones. As Fred always made him go to and fro in a straight line, he thought now he would go across the field in a zig-zag line – just for a change. Zig-zag, zig-zag, zig-zag he went. It was such fun that he clanked louder than ever, and puffed clouds of smoke out of his funnel.

When he had crossed to the far side of the field, he met some children from a farm. They were John and Jane and little Polly.

'Did you make this lovely zig-zag path through the thistles?' they asked him.

'Yes, I did,' said the Steam Roller.

'What for?' asked John.

'For you, if you like,' said the Steam Roller.

Then all the children jumped for joy and patted the Steam Roller so that it smiled.

'Thank you, thank you,' they cried. 'You have made us a lovely short cut to school. We've always had to go ALL round this big field because of the prickly thistles, and that often made us late for school. Now we can run along this lovely zig-zag path you have made. It will be our special short cut. Good-bye! We are going to school now. We will see you on the way home. Good-bye!'

The children ran off to school and the Steam Roller rested under a tree. He felt warm and sleepy. The bees were buzzing and the birds were singing, and he had a nap in the hot sunshine.

At tea-time, the children came back from school. They ran along the new flat, zig-zag path through the field of thistles. And they did not get their legs pricked at all. They were glad when they found the kind Steam Roller resting under a tree. 'Hullo, Steam Roller,' they said. 'Here we are again.'

Then they polished the Steam Roller's brasses till they shone like gold. They rubbed him all over with rags, and oiled him. They made chains of wild flowers and hung them round his funnel. He looked so smart and gay when they had finished that he smiled, and all his brasses winked in the sun.

'How nice I look now!' he said. 'Fred only wipes me over with an oily rag, but you've made me look like new.'

All that day, and through the night as well, Fred had been looking for his Steam Roller. He was thankful next day when he found him under the tree beside the thistle field.

'I am glad to see you again, old pal,' Fred said. 'I've been searching everywhere for you. I could not go to work without you, and the holes in the road have had to wait, and a milk cart fell into one of them, and there's been a lot of fuss about that. So we'd better be getting along! And you with flowers round your funnel! And aren't you smart with all your brasses shining!'

The Steam Roller was glad to see Fred again, and quite ready for work. He did not mind at all being driven back to the shed first because he was getting hungry and Fred gave him a good feed of coal. Fred filled his boiler with water too, and that was good because the Steam Roller was thirsty.

Next day, for a treat, Fred took the Steam Roller to work on a bridge over the river. As he went to and fro this time, the Steam Roller could look over the edge of the bridge and see the boats and barges go by. That was exciting, and the Steam Roller did not mind how often he had to go to and fro over that bit of road. It was almost like another holiday.

John and Jane and little Polly never forgot him,

because every day they ran along the zig-zag road he had cut across the thistles, and they were never late for school again. It was their special short cut.

A Doctor

THERE once was a doctor who said:
'Get up, child, and stand on your head!
   Turn head-over-heels,
   And do twenty cartwheels.
Don't snooze, like a dormouse, in bed!'

Charles and Dapple

ONE day, some new people came to live in the house next door to Charles. He saw the big furniture van stop outside and watched the men carrying in the chairs and carpets and beds. Then he saw them carry a dolls' house through the front door and a tricycle and a low table and chair.

'Oh, Mummy!' shouted Charles, running from the window into the kitchen. 'There's a little girl coming to live next door. I've seen some of her things. She has a tricycle just like mine.'

Charles did not see the little girl arrive, as she came in a car in the evening when he was going to bed, but next morning, when he was in the garden, he heard her voice. He stood beside the beech hedge and he heard her calling.

'Gee-up! Gee-up! Gee-up!' Then he heard the sound of a whip, crack, crack, and she called again, 'Gee-up! Gee-up, Dobbin! Gee-up, my fine horse.'

Charles listened hard, but he could not hear the sound of hoofs. Could there be a real live, pony next door, galloping round the lawn? If so, it was galloping very quietly. Perhaps the soft grass made it quiet.

Charles climbed on to the garden roller, which stood by the tool shed, and by standing on tip-toe he could peep over the hedge and see into the next garden. He could see the little girl galloping about on her horse and then he understood why there was no sound of hoofs. This horse had no feet. He was made of a broomstick and where the bristly part of the broom should be was a horse's head which looked like a sock stuffed with something.

The little girl had a leg each side of the stick and she galloped up and down, cracking a whip and calling to her horse.

Charles liked the horse's head. It was dark brown with two sharp brown ears and two big round eyes. The little girl saw him peeping over the hedge and she shouted 'Whoa! Whoa!' to her horse and stood still.

'Do you like my hobby horse?' she asked. 'I call him Dobbin. I've only had him a few days

and he knows his name and stops when I say
"Whoa!" and starts when I say "Gee-up!" and
crack my whip. Would you like to come into my
garden and have a ride?'

'Yes, I would,' said Charles. 'I can get through
the hedge in one place if I wriggle.' He soon
wriggled through and came out on the other
side with bits of twig and leaves in his hair. . . .
He had a lovely gallop on Dobbin. When they
were tired of riding, they put Dobbin in the sum-

mer house for a stable and gave him a bunch of
fresh green grass to munch.

In the afternoon, Charles asked his mother if
she could help him to make a hobby horse. They
found an old broom in the shed and took the
bristly end off. Then his mother got a grey wool
sock and Charles stuffed it tightly with rags. His
mother sewed on two more bits of sock for ears

and two big black buttons for eyes. Then she made some white stitches where the mouth was, to look like teeth. She tied the head very firmly on to the stick with a strong piece of string.

The little girl from next door, whose name was Pat, came and watched.

'Let's have a mane,' said Charles. 'A nice, long mane.'

'I'd like a mane on my horse, too,' said Pat. Mother found some thick, black wool and Charles and Pat cut it into pieces the same length and then mother sewed some on to Charles' horse and some on to Pat's horse.

Charles called his hobby horse Dapple and he and Pat had many good gallops together. Dobbin and Dapple went very well. 'Gee-up! Gee-up!' cried Charles and Pat and the horses started off. When they wanted to stop, they cried, 'Whoa! Whoa!' and the horses stopped at once.

They made reins of tape and threaded some curtain rings on. The rings jingled as the horses galloped, like real harness jingling.

'I should like a nose-bag for my horse,' said Charles. 'Horses always eat their dinners out of nose-bags so I want my Dapple to have one. A bag rather like my useful bag would do, but it does not need to draw up with a string. Dapple likes to put his nose right inside.'

Charles' mother made a nose-bag for Dapple and Pat's mother made a nose-bag for Dobbin. When it was dinner time, Charles and Pat filled the nose-bags with grass and hung them round the horses' necks. Then they could munch their food in their stable.

Sometimes, as a treat, Dobbin and Dapple were given an apple or a lump of sugar. If they did not seem hungry just then, can you guess what Charles and Pat did? Yes, they crunched the apple themselves. And the sugar, too.

Black Monkeys

ONE black monkey swinging on a tree.
Two black monkeys paddling in the sea.

Three black monkeys playing on a swing.
Four black monkeys dancing in a ring.

Five black monkeys drinking lemonade.
Six black monkeys digging with a spade.

Seven black monkeys wearing sailor hats.
Eight black monkeys waving cricket bats.

Nine black monkeys standing on their heads.
Ten black monkeys sleeping in their beds.

The Missing Present

MR and Mrs Plum were very busy. The curtains were drawn. The fire was burning brightly. Their five children were asleep in bed. There was nothing to disturb them.

The table and chairs had been pushed back against the walls to make a clear space in the middle of the room. In this space was a big wooden tub, painted dark green with red bands round it. In the tub was the tall Christmas tree that nearly reached the ceiling.

Mr and Mrs Plum were decorating the Christmas tree because it was Christmas Eve. First they put the candles in the metal holders. When the right time came, Mr Plum would light them with a long wax taper and they would shine like stars.

Then they put on the decorations, the bright baubles and the strings of gleaming tinsel and the gold and silver stars. There were little lanterns too, that the children had made themselves with coloured paper. There were crackers waiting to be pulled and opened. Even the smallest cracker had something pretty inside, a bead ring or a whistle or a lucky charm.

Then the tree was ready for the presents. There were so many of them that they filled a great clothes' basket. Five children were coming to tea on Christmas Day and with the five Plum children that made ten. Each child was to have two presents off the tree, so there had to be twenty presents.

Mrs Plum had been busy for days before, choosing the right things and writing the labels. She tied the bigger presents on the lower boughs and stood on a stool to hang the little ones higher up. Mr Plum tied the presents near the top. The tree was so tall that even he had to fetch a ladder to reach the little branches at the very tip.

On the tip top of all, he fixed a fairy doll with a silver wand and silver wings. She was not a present. She belonged to the Christmas tree and was brought out every Christmas Eve. She spent the rest of the year lying in a box, wrapped in black tissue paper to keep her silver bright.

When the clothes' basket was empty, Mrs Plum counted the presents on the tree. 'One, two, three, four,' she counted as she walked round the tree. 'Five, six, seven, eight.' When she got to nineteen, she stopped. 'Oh dear,' she said, 'we are one present short. We need twenty, and there are only nineteen.'

'Let *me* count,' said Mr Plum. 'I think we shall find there are twenty.' He counted very carefully, walking round and round the tree and muttering to himself, but there were only nineteen.

Then they counted out loud together, pointing to each present to make sure they did not miss one. Still there were only nineteen.

'What shall we do?' asked Mrs Plum. 'The shops are shut now, so we can't go out and buy another present. And I'm so busy with all the Christmas cooking that I shan't have a moment to make anything. Oh dear! Oh dear!'

'We'll think of something,' said Mr Plum cheerfully. 'Let's look in the toy chest. We may get an idea.'

The toy chest was a wooden box on wheels. It was full of all kinds of toys, mostly old and shabby. There were stuffed animals who had lost an eye or an ear. There were dolls with torn dresses and trucks with only three wheels. There were farm animals that would not stand straight.

Suddenly Mr Plum dived down to the very bottom of the box and brought out a little wooden rocking horse. His paint had worn off so that no one could tell what colour he had been when he was new. He was scratched and scraped and chipped. But his two ears stood up, stiff and jointed, and he could still rock up and down.

'He's a nice little fellow,' said Mr Plum. 'A new coat of paint and a new tail and he'll look a treat.'

The little rocking horse felt so excited that he nearly choked. He had lain so long at the bottom of the toy chest that he had given up hope of ever being played with again.

Mr Plum stood him on a sheet of newspaper on the table and got out three pots of paint to paint him black and white with red spots. Rocking horses usually have spots on them, and his rockers were painted red. Then Mrs Plum left the cooking to make him a fine plaited tail of black wool, and when it was stuck on, he was finished.

He stood on the mantelpiece all night to get dry, and next morning – Christmas morning – Mrs Plum tied a label on his neck and Mr Plum fixed him to a branch on the tree – not too high, for he was no very light weight. He had a good view of the room with paper chains hung across and holly behind the pictures.

After a good Christmas tea, Mr Plum lit the candles on the tree with the long wax taper and the children came dancing into the room in a long line.

'Oh!' they all cried together. 'Oh, isn't it *beautiful*! It is the most beautiful Christmas tree in all the whole world!'

Then Mr Plum took the presents off the tree, one by one, and gave them to the children, first one each, and then round again, so that each child had two presents. The little rocking horse was given to a boy called Peter. Peter's other present was a screw-up pencil, but he liked the rocking horse best. He stroked him and patted him and rocked him up and down.

'I shall call you "Rocker",' said Peter.

The little rocking horse rocked gently up and down with happiness. Now that he had red spots and a red rocker and the new tail Mrs Plum had made him and a new name as well, what more could any little horse want?

Granny in the Country

CHARLES was very lucky because he had two grandmothers. One lived by the sea and he called her 'granny-by-the-sea'. The other lived in the country and he called her 'granny-in-the-country'. Sometimes he went with his mother to visit his grannies and sometimes he stayed all by himself for a few days.

Granny-in-the-country lived in a cottage. She had a garden where Charles could play and there was a lane with green hedges just outside the gate. His mother took him by train to the nearest station and there granny met him. She had a little pony trap outside, drawn by Peggy the pony, and she lifted Charles' suitcase inside and then Charles, carrying his useful bag himself, climbed up and sat beside her.

'Gee-up, Peggy pony,' said granny. 'Gee-up!' and Peggy tossed her head and set off at a gentle clip-clop, clip-clop, along the lane.

'May I hold the reins, please?' asked Charles.

'Yes, for a little while,' said granny and Charles sat up very straight and still, holding the leather reins tightly. The leather had a smell like new shoes.

When they got to the cottage, Charles climbed down from the trap and ran up the path, swinging his useful bag by the strings. The cottage was exactly the same as he remembered. The door stood open, with a horse-shoe nailed on it for a knocker. There was a fire burning and the kettle was singing. There was a smell of new scones. Charles hung his bag on the back of a chair and ran outside again.

'Granny! Granny! Can I give Peggy pony a drink of water?'

'Yes,' said granny, who was undoing Peggy's harness. 'I'll help you.'

There was a well near the back door with a heavy cover over the top. Granny moved the cover and helped Charles to turn the handle so that the bucket, on the end of the rope, went down, down into the water. It made a splash when it got there. Winding the handle back again was difficult now there was a heavy bucket of water to be lifted, but they managed it be-

tween them. They gave Peggy a drink and she
dipped her soft nose in and gulped the cool
water. When she had had enough, she lifted her
head and whinnied. Charles tried to whinny back
but he did not do it very well.

There were hot buttered scones for tea and a
special mug for Charles with daisies painted
round it. At the very bottom, on the inside, was

the picture of a cow. Granny poured milk into the daisy mug and as he drank it up he watched for the picture of the cow to appear. When he was near the bottom he saw first her head and then her back and then her legs. This made it easy to finish every drop. He never left any of his milk when he was staying with granny-in-the-country.

When Charles was in bed he asked granny to tell him just one little story before he went to sleep.

'Of course I will,' said granny. 'Which story do you want to hear?'

'Please tell about Peggy pony in the snow,' said Charles. So granny began:

'One wintry day when the snow was on the ground, I went to the stable to give Peggy pony her breakfast. "Here's a nice hot breakfast for you," I said, as I came down the path. Then I saw that the stable door was wide open and I looked inside and saw the straw on the floor, but no Peggy pony. Where could she be on such a cold and frosty morning? Had a thief come in the night and stolen her away?

'Then I saw a trail of hoof-marks in the snow

and I followed the hoof-marks out of the gate and along the lane and over the bridge and past the post office. Then they swung round into the blacksmith's forge and as I followed them I heard the clang-clang-clang of the blacksmith's hammer and I heard something else too. I heard Peggy pony's whinny. And there stood Peggy inside the forge, holding up one of her back feet so patiently while the blacksmith fitted a bright new shoe on it.

' "Clever lass! Clever lass, your Peggy!" said the blacksmith smiling. "I heard her whinnying outside in the snow and I opened my door and in she trotted. What can I do for you? I asked and she held up her foot to show that she'd cast a shoe. So I've made her a new one, as you can see.'

'Wasn't that clever of Peggy pony? Then I got on her back and paid the blacksmith for the new shoe and we rode home. Then Peggy had her breakfast rather late.

'When the snow melted, I found the old shoe she had lost by the gate.'

'Is it the one nailed on the door for a knocker?' asked Charles sleepily.

'Yes, the very same one. And when she casts another shoe you shall have it to nail on *your* door, at home.'

By this time, Charles was very nearly asleep but as he knew every word of the story by heart it did not matter. Granny would tell him the same story the next night and the next night and the one after that, until he asked for a new one.

Winkle and the Christmas Tree

TABBY CAT and her three kittens slept in a box under the kitchen table. When the kittens grew bigger and their legs became stronger, Tabby Cat sometimes took them for a walk into the dining-room, or the sitting-room, or the hall.

In the dining-room was a gas fire which hissed and had an angry red face. Winkle, who was the bravest of the kittens, hissed back at it.

In the hall was a row of shoes and slippers. The kittens played with the shoe laces and sometimes, when they were tired, they crept into a slipper and fell asleep there because it was so warm and soft, like a cradle.

When it was almost Christmas time, a tall green Christmas tree was brought into the hall, and hung with pretty lights and glass balls and presents done up in gay paper. On the top a Fairy Doll was perched with a silver wand in her hand.

The kittens could do nothing but stare at the beautiful tree.

'May we climb it?' they asked.

'May we bite it?'

'May we lick the candles?'

'Shall we get one of those presents?' they asked.

But Mother Cat's answer to all those questions was 'NO'.

'You may *look*,' said Tabby Cat, 'and that is all. The tree is for the children, not for you. You might, if you were good, have a special present each, but you will find it beside your box when you wake up on Christmas morning.'

Winkle was not content with just looking. He wanted to sniff with his little black nose, and to lick with his small pink tongue, and to touch with his furry paws. So that night, when his two sisters and Tabby Cat were all asleep, he crept softly out of the box and crossed the kitchen floor. He tip-toed into the hall, scrambled up the side of the tub in which the Christmas tree was planted, and began very carefully to climb up.

Climbing was not as nice as he had expected. The branches of the tree were springy and difficult to cling to, and the thin pointed leaves pricked his nose. His feet caught in the strings of tinsel and paper chains. But he kept on, and at last he reached the top, and found his little damp nose almost touching the golden hair and smooth pink cheeks of the Fairy Doll.

'A happy Christmas!' said the Fairy Doll. 'You are the first kitten who has ever climbed our Christmas tree.'

'A happy Christmas!' replied Winkle. 'You are the first Fairy Doll I have ever spoken to.'

'But you must get down at once, before your mother wakes up and misses you,' said the Fairy Doll. 'Go carefully. You might spoil something if you slipped.'

Winkle went very carefully, but he had to go down head first and that made him feel very dizzy. When he was half-way down, his paws slipped away from a prickly branch. He clutched at a candle to save himself, but the wax was too smooth and slippery for him to hold. He caught at a string of tinsel for a moment – but the string broke. He leaped at a glass ball and rocked on it

till it fell off the tree and smashed on the floor into a thousand splinters.

Winkle fell as well, but he landed on the soft earth inside the tub, and was not hurt.

He picked himself up, and shook himself from his ears right down to the tip of his tail. Then he looked at the broken glass ball. No one could mend it, he was sure. It had been like a lovely shining bubble of a ball. Now it lay on the floor, a thousand jagged scraps of fine glass.

Winkle looked up at the Fairy Doll and mewed sadly:

'Please help me, Fairy Doll! Please help me! Please put the broken ball together again. I know you can with your magic wand. Please try.'

'I will try,' said the Fairy Doll, 'but I don't think I can do anything as difficult as that.'

She spread her fairy wings and flew down from her high branch, and waved her silver wand over the broken glass ball.

Nothing happened.

'Try harder,' mewed Winkle.

'Try harder,' the Fairy Doll whispered to her wand, and she waved it twice.

Still nothing happened.

Then she gave the wand a shake and said crossly:

'You *must* try harder, *much* harder! You must make more magic. You are no better than a clothes' peg.'

The magic wand did not like to be scolded, so the third time the Fairy Doll waved it, it tried very hard indeed, and the tiny glass splinters swept themselves together and made a shining glass ball again, as good as new.

'Thank you, oh, thank you,' purred Winkle, as the Fairy Doll flew up and hung the glass ball in its proper place on the tree.

When the kittens woke up next morning, they found their presents lying on the kitchen rug beside their bed. There was a ping-pong ball for each of them – and what fun they were! The three ping-pong balls rolled all over the floor, and the kittens went chasing after them. Tabby Cat was kept busy hooking them out with her paw from under cupboards and inside the fender.

Winkle never tried to climb the Christmas tree again, but he always waved his tail to the Fairy Doll when he went into the hall, and she waved her wand back. And when he saw the shining glass ball, he purred to himself and thought that that was his secret – his and the Fairy Doll's.

RIDDLES

What thing am I?

I HAVE legs,
One, two, three, four,
But I cannot walk
Across the floor.

Answer: A CHAIR

I HAVE teeth,
Long and white,
They are sharp
But I cannot bite.

Answer: A COMB

I CAN prick your finger
And make you cry,
But I can't see a thing
With my one little eye.

Answer: A NEEDLE

Other Young Puffins

THE TEN TALES OF SHELLOVER *Ruth Ainsworth*

The Black Hens, the Dog and the Cat didn't like Shellover the tortoise at first, until they discovered what wonderful stories he told.

LITTLE PETE STORIES *Leila Berg*

More favourites from *Listen With Mother*, about a small boy who plays mostly by himself. Illustrated by Peggy Fortnum.

HERE COMES THURSDAY *Michael Bond*

THURSDAY RIDES AGAIN

THURSDAY AHOY!

THURSDAY IN PARIS

The mouse arrived on Thursday, so that's what he was named when he was adopted by the Pecks, the church mice, and became their twentieth child.

THE CASTLE OF YEW *Lucy M. Boston*

Joseph visits the magic garden where the yew trees are shaped like castles – and finds himself shrunk small enough to crawl inside one.

THE HAPPY ORPHELINE *Natalie Savage Carlson*

The twenty little orphaned girls who live with Madame Flattot are terrified of being adopted because they are so happy.

A BROTHER FOR THE ORPHELINES *Natalie Savage Carlson*

Josine finds a baby boy on the doorstep, and the orphans plot and worry to find a way of keeping him.

FIVE DOLLS IN A HOUSE *Helen Clare*

A little girl called Elizabeth finds a way of making herself small and visits her dolls in their own house.

TELL ME A STORY *Eileen Colwell*

TELL ME ANOTHER STORY

TIME FOR A STORY

Stories, verses, and finger plays for children of 3 to 6, collected by the greatest living expert on the art of children's story-telling.

MY NAUGHTY LITTLE SISTER *Dorothy Edwards*
MY NAUGHTY LITTLE SISTER'S FRIENDS
WHEN MY NAUGHTY LITTLE SISTER WAS GOOD

These now famous stories were originally told by a mother to her own children. Ideal for reading aloud. For ages 4 to 8.

MISS HAPPINESS AND MISS FLOWER *Rumer Godden*

Nona was lonely far away from her home in India, and the two dainty Japanese dolls, Miss Happiness and Miss Flower, were lonely too. But once Nona started building them a proper Japanese house they all felt happier. Illustrated by Jean Primrose.

THREE LITTLE FUNNY ONES *Charlotte Hough*

Oliver, Timmy and Tom have some adventures which are just frightening enough to make them interesting, like when they make a lion trap and catch a sausage dog. (Also available in Initial Teaching Alphabet.)

THE STORY OF FERDINAND *Munro Leaf*

The endearing story of the adventures of the nicest bull there ever was – and it has a very happy ending.

MEET MARY KATE *Helen Morgan*

Charmingly told stories of a four-year-old's everyday life in the country. Illustrated by Shirley Hughes.

PUFFIN BOOK OF NURSERY RHYMES *Peter and Iona Opie*

The first comprehensive collection of nursery rhymes to be produced as a paperback, prepared for Puffins by the leading authorities on children's lore. 220 pages, exquisitely illustrated on every page by Pauline Baynes. (*A Young Puffin Original*.)

LITTLE OLD MRS PEPPERPOT *Alf Prøysen*
MRS PEPPERPOT TO THE RESCUE
MRS PEPPERPOT IN THE MAGIC WOOD
MRS PEPPERPOT'S OUTING

Gay little stories about an old woman who suddenly shrinks to the size of a pepperpot.

ROM-BOM-BOM AND OTHER STORIES *Antonia Ridge*

A collection of animal stories written by the distinguished children's author and broadcaster. For 4- to 8-year-olds.

DEAR TEDDY ROBINSON *Joan G. Robinson*
ABOUT TEDDY ROBINSON
TEDDY ROBINSON HIMSELF
KEEPING UP WITH TEDDY ROBINSON

Teddy Robinson was Deborah's teddy bear and such a very nice, friendly cuddly bear that he went everywhere with her and had even more adventures than she did.

THE ADVENTURES OF GALLDORA *Modwena Sedgwick*

This lovable rag doll belonged to Marybell, who wasn't always very careful to look after her, so Galldora was always getting lost – in a field with a scarecrow, on top of a roof, and in all sorts of other strange places.

SOMETHING TO DO *Septima*

Suggestions for games to play and things to make and do each month, from January to December. It is designed to help mothers with young children at home. (*A Young Puffin Original.*)

PONDER AND WILLIAM *Barbara Softly*
PONDER AND WILLIAM ON HOLIDAY

Ponder the panda looks after William's pyjamas and is a wonderful companion in these all the year round adventures. Illustrated by Diana John. (*A Young Puffin Original.*)

CLEVER POLLY AND THE STUPID WOLF *Catherine Storr*

Clever Polly manages to think of lots of good ideas to stop the stupid wolf from eating her.

DANNY FOX *David Thomson*

Clever Danny Fox helps the Princess to marry the fisherman she loves and comes safely home to his hungry family. (*A Young Puffin Original.*)

DANNY FOX MEETS A STRANGER *David Thomson*

The stranger was a big grey wolf, and he tried to steal Danny's den and his hunting grounds.

THE URCHIN *Edith Unnerstad*

The Urchin is only five years old – but already he has the Larsson family at sixes and sevens with his ingenious tricks and adventures.

LITTLE O *Edith Unnerstad*

The enchanting story of the youngest of the Pip Larsson family.

MAGIC IN MY POCKET *Alison Uttley*

A selection of short stories by this well-loved author, especially good for 5- and 6-year-olds.

LITTLE RED FOX *Alison Uttley*
MORE LITTLE RED FOX STORIES

Little Red Fox is adopted by kind Mr and Mrs Badger, but finds it hard to be as good as their own children.

THE PENNY PONY *Barbara Willard*

Life is never quite the same for Cathy and Roger after they find the penny pony in Mrs Boddy's shop. A delightful story for readers of six to eight.

GOBBOLINO THE WITCH'S CAT *Ursula Moray Williams*

Gobbolino's mother was ashamed of him because his eyes were blue instead of green, and he wanted to be loved instead of learning spells. So he goes in search of a friendly kitchen. Illustrated by the author.

ADVENTURES OF THE LITTLE WOODEN HORSE
Ursula Moray Williams

To help his master, a brave little horse sets out to sell himself and brings home a great fortune.